This Walker book belongs to:

First published 2002 by Walker Books Ltd
87 Vauxhall Walk, London SE11 5HJ

This edition published 2011

2 4 6 8 10 9 7 5 3 1

This book has been typeset in Stone Informal

Printed in China

British Library Cataloguing in Publication Data:
a catalogue record for this book is available from the British Library

ISBN 978-1-4063-3297-1

www.walker.co.uk

ALL FOR ONE

JILL MURPHY

WALKER BOOKS
AND SUBSIDIARIES
LONDON • BOSTON • SYDNEY • AUCKLAND

Marlon had run out of things to do. He had done lots of drawing …

and built a secret cave out of the sofa cushions.

He had made a big castle
out of the videos, blown
it up with his special
alien powers ...

and helped his army on a dangerous mission up the bookcase.

"I wish I had someone to play with," said Marlon.
"I can't think of anything else to do."
"Well," said Marlon's granny, "you can tidy up this room for a start. It looks as if a bomb's hit it."
"A bomb *has* hit it," said Marlon. "My alien space

bomb blew everything up."

"Don't be ridiculous," said Marlon's mum. "Come on, I'll help you tidy up, then you can see who's out playing – there might be a game you could join in. I'll do the cushions."

"OK," said Marlon. "I'll do the videos."

Marlon went outside and found Basher, Boomps-a-daisy and Alligatina all bashing each other with swords.

"What are you playing?" asked Marlon.

"The Three Musketeers," said Boomps-a-daisy.

"Can *I* play?" asked Marlon.

"No," said Basher. "There's only *three* musketeers, can't you count? There aren't *four*."

"Yes there are," said Marlon. "There's four when that other one joins in later. I could be the other one, and their motto *is* 'All for One—'"

"And One for All except Marlon!" sneered Alligatina.

"Can't I play anyway?" pleaded Marlon.

"We'll think about it," said Basher.

Marlon rushed home.
"I've got to be a musketeer, Mum!" he said.
"If I get dressed up, they might let me play!"

Marlon put on a big T-shirt and his mum made him a cloak out of an old curtain. His granny lent him a hat she had worn to a wedding. Marlon put his best sword into his belt and pulled on his wellington boots.

“Perfect!” said his mum.

Marlon ran back to the others.
"Here I am!" he said.

"We aren't musketeers any more," explained Boomps-a-daisy. "We're pirates now."

"I can see that," said Marlon.

"He could be the cabin-boy," said Alligatina.

"Can I?" said Marlon. "Pleeeease."

"We'll think about it," said Basher.

Marlon rushed back home.
"I've got to be a pirate now!"
he shouted. "Quick!"

Marlon's mum found a scarf and sewed some curtain rings onto it. She made him an eye patch, and Marlon put on his striped T-shirt with a cutlass in his belt.
"Brilliant!" said his mum.

Marlon raced back to the others.
"Here I am!" he said.

But the others weren't pirates any more. They were doing handstands and swinging on the climbing frame.

"What are you doing now?" asked Marlon.

"We're having a gymnastic contest," said Basher.

"We're not doing pirates any more."

Marlon gave up. He wasn't very good at gymnastic contests, especially ones with Basher in them.

"What's the matter, love?" asked Marlon's mum as he mooched into the kitchen.
"They keep changing the game," said Marlon – "Can we fill up the new paddling pool?"
"It's a bit chilly out," said Marlon's mum.
"We could fill it with warm water," said Marlon.
"Pleeeeeeeease?"

"He'll catch a cold," warned Granny. "He'll freeze to death in a paddling pool in this weather."

Marlon's mum looked at Marlon, all dressed up in his pirate outfit and no one to play with.

"All right, then," she said. "Go and get your swimming things."

"You spoil that little monster," muttered Marlon's granny.

While Marlon changed into his swimming things,
his mum fixed the garden hose to the kitchen tap
and filled the pool until it began to steam in the cold air.

Marlon's granny watched from the window. "This is ridiculous," she said. "In my day we just sat quietly and read a book."

Marlon leapt in.
"I'm a famous underwater explorer," he said.
"I'm hunting the rare and extremely dangerous giant pink starfish!"

Marlon's granny brought him
a drink and a piece of cake.
"We don't want him starving
as well as freezing," she said.

Then it began to rain, so Marlon's
mum fixed up an umbrella to
stop the cake going soggy.

On their way home, Alligatina, Boomps-a-daisy
and Basher looked over the wall.

"What a cool pool," said Alligatina. "It's really big."

"We could all get in there with you," said Boomps-a-daisy.

"What are you playing?" asked Basher.
"Underwater explorers," said Marlon.
"I wish we'd thought of that," said Basher.
"Can we come and play tomorrow?"

Marlon leaned back and took a sip of orange juice.

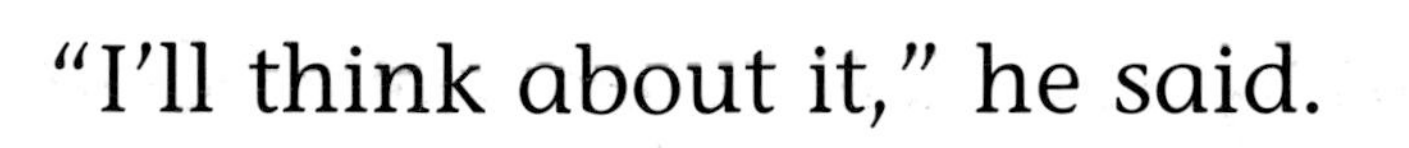

"I'll think about it," he said.

Another book about Marlon by Jill Murphy

ISBN 978-1-4063-3184-4

Also available *The Large Family*

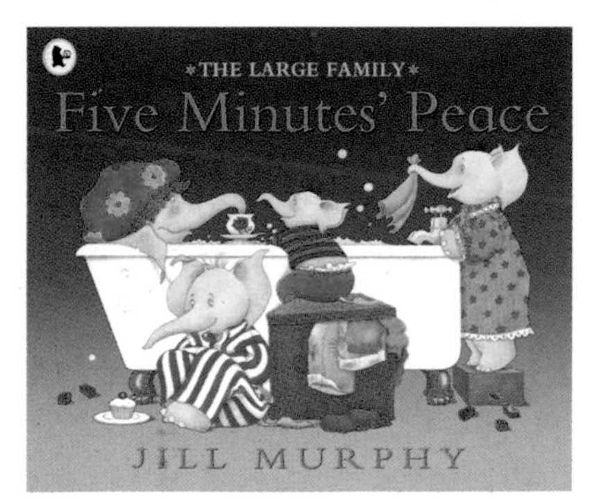

ISBN 978-1-84428-539-6

ISBN 978-1-84428-534-1

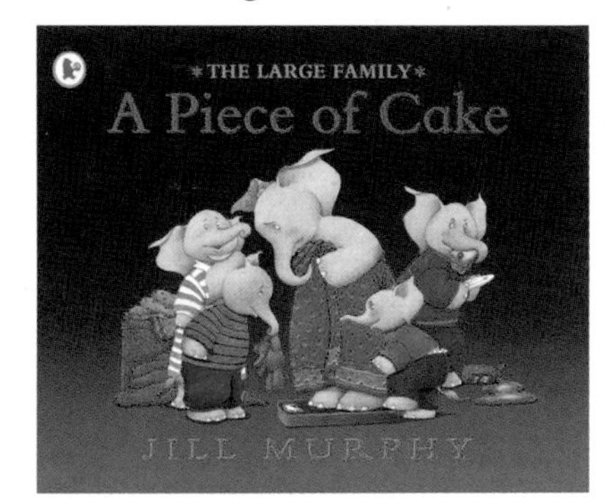

ISBN 978-1-84428-526-6

ISBN 978-1-84428-527-3

ISBN 978-1-4063-0074-1

Available from all good bookstores

www.walker.co.uk